THE CHRISTMAS CAT

By
James T. Huckleberry
Illustrated by
Carolyn Seabolt

Bookman LLC
Publishing & Marketing

Providing Quality, Professional
Author Services

www.bookmanmarketing.com

INTRODUCTION

This book is dedicated to Peppy our family cat. The events described occurred on Christmas Eve and Christmas Day several years ago.

A picture of Peppy today is somewhere in this book. See if you can find him.

Also a special thank you goes to Carolyn Seabolt whose wonderful artwork brings a true story to life.

There he sat,

the Christmas cat,

watching snowflakes fall.

Let outside,

he pranced and danced

at all the wetness

on his paws.

Alert, awake,

with perfect sight,

he didn't catch

a single flake.

James T. Huckleberry

Wet and cold,

he came inside

and snoozed away

a trying day.

James T. Huckleberry

I later spied

the Christmas cat

beneath a lighted tree.

Content to lie,

sometimes he'd play

while purring oh so noisily.

From time to time,

he'd stretch and yawn

to Jingle Bells or Tannenbaum.

He'd swat the tinsel

to and fro,

or try to untie another bow.

There he lay,

the Christmas cat,

late on Christmas Eve.

No one about,

with all lights out,

he quickly went to sleep.

Santa grinned

from ear to ear.

No Christmas Cat

would catch him here.

He laid a ball

between his paws,

just before

he disappeared.

I watched him stretch,

the Christmas cat,

early Christmas morn.

He sniffed the ball,

rolled it down the hall,

and batted it all around.

What a day

And feast it was.

A goose was cooked.

He ate of that.

He then curled up

And went to sleep,

One contented Christmas cat.

James T. Huckleberry

This is a picture of Peppy today.

We hope you enjoyed the story.

Merry Christmas.

ABOUT THE AUTHOR

Born in Olympia, Washington, the author has traveled extensively through his military and civil service career. He resides in Middletown, Maryland with his wife. They have four children and three grandchildren. The author has a Masters Degree from the University of Northern Colorado and is an avid skier. The author has one published poetry book entitled "Hidden Feelings Die Unspoken". His poems have been published by World Book of Poetry, The National Book of Poetry, The International Library of Poetry, Noble House and Famous Poets Press.